Holler Presents
STORIES V!
2011

Stories V!
Copyright 2011 Scott McClanahan
All Rights Reserved
First Edition: February 2011
Manufactured in the United States
ISBN: 978-0-9832589-6-4

Front Cover Design by Holler Presents
Book layout by sunnyoutside

Holler Presents
110 Hale Street
Beckley, WV
25801

scottmcclanahan@hotmail.com
hollerpresents@gmail.com

For Sarah

STORIES V!

Scott McClanahan

STORIES V!

Invisible Ink	9
Jenny Sugar	17
Terrorists	29
The Second Ending to Terrorists	41
A Chapter from a Book I Will Start Writing in 2012	45
Sex Tapes	49
But There Is a Second Ending to Sex Tapes Too	65
And Now a Note on Literary Reverence	69
So Now A List of Things I'm Ashamed of	71
Nicky	73
Now Some Public Apologies	85
Love Letters	87
Razy	89
Dead Baby Jokes	99
Mary the Cleaning Lady	123
A Farewell	137

INVISIBLE INK

WHEN I WAS A CHILD my mother wrote me a note in invisible ink. I took it from her hands and there was nothing on it. It was just a piece of paper.

She said, "It's magic. I wrote it in invisible ink. Just wait."

So I held it in my hands for a couple of minutes and she asked me, "Do you believe?"

I nodded my head, "Yeah."

I waited a few more seconds and then a message appeared.

It said, "Thank you for believing."

✳

So I have decided to write a whole book in invisible ink. If you believe enough and if the invisible ink truly works then it will appear in a few pages.

So I ask you now, "Do you believe?"

THANK YOU FOR BELIEVING.

JENNY SUGAR

I WAS IN THE FOURTH GRADE when this little girl in my class got killed.

I showed up at school one Monday morning and Randy Doogan was telling me all about it, "Hey Scott did you hear about Jenny Sugar? She got killed in a car crash yesterday. Yeah a tractor trailer hit her Mom's car and they're both dead."

Of course, I didn't believe him at first because Randy Doogan was always making up stuff up like this. He was always going on about how his Dad lived in England, even though this was just something his Mother told him because his Dad left them and never came back.

But he just kept going on about it. "My Mom saw it on the news last night and she's dead."

Then he giggled and moved on to the next kids sitting at the cafeteria tables, "Hey guys did you hear about Jenny Sugar and her mom? They got killed yesterday?"

I stood and giggled too not really knowing what was going on and wondering if it was true or not.

But it was true all right. We found out just a couple of minutes later from our fourth grade teacher, Mrs. Morgan. She stood in front of our class and told us that Jenny and her Mother had been visiting Jenny's grandma in Virginia. On the way back home Jenny's Mom was driving behind this tractor trailer. Jenny's Mom was passing it on the right hand side of the road, but as she was passing it the truck pulled over and the car crashed beneath the truck. The driver kept driving because he didn't know what happened.

The tractor trailer driver drove for another five minutes before he finally realized he was dragging a car beneath him.

So after telling us this, Mrs. Morgan sat down at her desk and put her head in her hands. We were supposed to be working on our spelling words like 'F-R-I-E-N-D-S' and 'M-O-T-H-E-R' but everybody just stopped and watched her. She sat for a second and then she started to cry. It wasn't your typical sad cry now, but it was a cry that sounded different.

It was a cry a woman would cry if she wasn't our teacher Mrs. Morgan anymore, but a thirty five-year-old woman named Elaine.

I put my pencil down and listened to her cry and thought, "Yes. Hallelujah! We're not gonna have to do any work today!"

Then another girl named Tina started crying too.

So Mrs. Morgan walked over and asked her if she needed to go to the bathroom.

Tina nodded her head yeah.

Mrs. Morgan touched Tina's shoulder and asked Nicole to go to the bathroom with her.

I leaned over and told my friend Mike, "What's up with that? She didn't even know her that well."

But inside my head I was just jealous because I wished I could be free too.

Finally Mrs. Morgan was able to compose herself and told us all, "I know this is a horrible accident but there is going to be a funeral tomorrow and I hope we can all go. I have permission forms you need your parents to sign tonight if you wish to go. I'll also be calling each of your parents tonight."

She said if it was too much for anyone, we could just stay behind and Mrs. Crookshanks would be showing a movie.

Somebody raised their hand and asked, "What movie?"

Mrs. Morgan said she didn't know. She thought maybe a Superman movie.

I didn't say anything but I was thinking –
Superman or the funeral?
Superman or the funeral?
I picked the Superman movie.

The next day at school it seemed like everybody else picked the funeral. Dumb bastards. They got on the bus all dressed up in their nice shirts and ties and church dresses and church shoes. We watched from the window as they got on the school bus and took off.

There were only a couple of us who didn't go that day. There was me, and Debra the retarded girl. And there was Kevin Van Meter, the kid who always pooped his pants. He wanted to go too, but since he always pooped his pants the teacher just made up an excuse so he couldn't go.

After they all left, we sat in the dark classroom and Mrs. Crookshanks put *Superman IV* in the VCR. I sat and watched and there was a part of me saying, "This is great. This is two days in a row we haven't had to do any work. I mean who'd go off to a dumb funeral when there's Superman playing?"

But after only watching a half hour of *Superman IV*, I realized something important.

Superman IV sucked. *Superman IV* really sucked.

You could see the wires that were holding Christopher Reeve up in the air, and the microphone was showing in one shot. Then all of the sudden Debra, the retarded girl, started crying.

I was like, "Debra, shhh, or they're going to turn off the movie."

So she finally quit crying. But *Superman IV* wasn't getting any better and to make matters worse I started smelling something.

I sniffed my nose a couple of times and then I turned to Kevin Van Meter and told him, "Did you just poop your pants?"

Kevin Van Metter kept looking at *Superman IV* and said, "No I didn't."

"Yes you did."

"No I didn't."

"Yes you did. I can smell it. You crapped your pants like you always do. It's no wonder they wouldn't let you go to the funeral."

Finally Kevin Van Meter raised his hand and did what he always did. He raised his hand and said in his deep, speech impediment voice, "I'm telling teacher on you."

The teacher came over and Kevin told her, "Teacher, he picking on me."

But Mrs. Crookshanks smelled him too and instead of yelling at me, she just turned off the VCR and took Kevin to the bathroom.

Shit.

We didn't even get to watch the end of the movie.

It wasn't an hour later the school bus pulled back up in front of the school and they were back. They were all dressed up in shirts and ties, and nice dresses and for some reason or other they didn't look happy. I even tried telling my best friend Matt Chapman about how *Superman IV* sucked and how he should be happy he went to the funeral.

"I mean, Matt, it was horrible," I said as he looked away from me.

I laughed. "I mean you could actually see the cables holding him up in a couple of shots."

But Matt didn't say anything to me.

He just looked at me all disgusted.

I said, "How come you're acting like this and not saying anything?"

Matt shook his head and said, "I just came back from a funeral Scott. I don't care about some stupid movie that my Mom can rent for me down at Country Boys. And how come you didn't go? What's wrong with you?"

I thought, "What do you mean why didn't I go?"

But then he gave me a look I'd never seen before. It was the kind of look like my Dad gave me when I was doing something wrong. It was a grown-up look.

For the rest of the day I sat at my desk thinking about how *Superman IV* sucked and then I started thinking about Jenny Sugar.

I thought about how a couple of weeks earlier my Mother took a picture of her at a school carnival and she didn't smile. She didn't smile because she was embarrassed.

She'd just started wearing braces. I thought

about the last time I saw her. We were both outside cleaning out our fourth grade lockers and I was trying to make her laugh by doing a funny voice.

"Hee Hee," I laughed in my funny voice, but she didn't laugh.

"Maybe she didn't hear me," I thought.

So I did it again, "Hee hee."

She rolled her eyes, and shook her head, and went "Ugghhh" like I was so immature. Maybe I was.

But in the next couple of weeks it was like the rest of the kids completely forgot about Jenny Sugar. It was like they were the ones who stayed behind and watched Superman instead of saying goodbye. It was like it never even happened. It wasn't even a week later and they were all laughing again, and doing fart jokes and playing touch football at recess.

I kept asking, "Isn't it strange that Jenny's gone? What was the funeral like? Were people crying?"

They acted like they didn't even know what I was talking about. And then one day doing my spelling words I came across a word.

It was spelled, 'S-K-E-L-E-T-O-N.' Skeleton.

So I stopped doing them.

I looked around and all the other kids were spelling 'S-K-E-L-E-T-O-N' like there was nothing wrong with it.

I went to the bathroom and passed two teachers in the hallway talking about Jenny's death.

They said, "I think they're holding up pretty well. It's just so horrible what happened." And then the other teacher whispered like she didn't want anyone to hear, "Well you can't even imagine it. I heard the little girl was decapitated and that's why they had a closed coffin. Imagine the father losing his wife and only child in the same day. I know he quit drinking when she was born. I wonder what will happen to him now?"

I kept thinking about it.

I thought about Jenny Sugar without her head.

I thought about closed caskets.

I thought about Jenny Sugar's skeleton and blood.

Each morning I woke up and my stomach was hurting.

I was in the bathroom so much my Mom started getting worried.

"Are you okay in there Scott?" she asked through the door.

"Yeah I'm fine," I said. "My belly's just a little upset."

"You want me to get you some more Pepto?"

I said, "Yes, Mam," but I kept thinking about it.

I thought about it so much that by the time school was over that summer I couldn't even get into my Mother's car. My Mom and I were supposed to visit my Grandma in Virginia, but I was dreading it. I hung out all summer getting even more scared, drinking Pepto Bismol, worrying about how I wasn't baptized yet, and wondering how I was going to tell her I didn't want to go to Virginia. I didn't want to go anywhere. I wasn't baptized yet. If I died, I would be stuck in hell. I didn't want to get in a car and get killed by a tractor trailer. I didn't want to get decapitated like Jenny. I didn't want to wind up stuck in hell like Jenny. This went on for weeks.

Then on the day we were supposed to leave I sat in the car and I told her, "I don't want to go Mom. I really don't want to go."

And at first my Mom was mad, "Scott we're supposed to be leaving. Why didn't you tell me this a couple of weeks ago?"

Then it dawned on her that I was afraid. I was afraid something was going to happen to us.

I sat in the car and cried, "Why did Jenny have to get killed that way and lose her head?"

She shrugged and said, "I don't know."

I asked, "Where is she now Mom? Why did Jenny get her head cut off?"

She said, "I don't know Scott."

She was telling the truth. I was shaking now.

I said, "I don't want to go because I don't want something bad to happen. I don't want to be a skeleton."

My Mom thought for a second and said, "Nothing bad is going to happen to us. I won't let anything happen to you. There's nothing going to happen to us. I won't let it happen to us. I promise."

I was feeling better.

And then she said it again as we pulled away, "Don't you worry about that now. We're not going to get killed. There's nothing bad EVER going to happen to us. I won't let it."

✳

I wasn't crying anymore. My mother was a fucking liar.

TERRORISTS

OF COURSE, I KNEW what people were thinking. It was a few months after 9-11 and I wanted to protect them. That day I was sitting in my office at school when they showed up, wearing their traditional head coverings—the hijab, and asking for help with their English skills.

Alima was older and had moved to West Virginia after her arranged marriage to a local doctor's brother. Sabah, her sister, was unmarried and they were both only a month away from their home in Lebanon. I tried talking to them, but they were so nervous they just kept looking down at the ground and nodding their heads politely. It was five minutes before they were able to explain who they were and how they wanted me to help them with their writing.

They said, "We speak well but our, but our, writing is bad."

So I had them sit down at the table and we started working.

I said, "Okay, I want you to write a sentence in English, any English sentence you can think of."

I watched them listening to my directions and working it out in their heads. I watched them listening to my directions in English, translating them into Arabic, thinking of a sentence in Arabic and then translating that back into English before finally writing it down on the paper. Man.

I read the sentences and corrected them.

Then we talked about it, and I asked, "Do you understand what I just said?"

They smiled and nodded, "Yes."

We did it again. I asked them to speak the sentence out loud and then write down what they were saying. This would make it easier for them.

I said, "Do you understand what I'm talking about?"

They shook their heads and said, "Yes."

I said, "You have no clue what I'm talking about do you?"

They smiled and shook their heads, "Yes."

Over the next couple of weeks we kept working and they started making progress. They were writing better, even catching their own mistakes, and now we were talking more. We started talking about personal stuff—who we were. I learned how they came from a group of desert people called the Bedouins. I mentioned one of my favorite films *Lawrence of Arabia*, and then one of my favorite books *The Seven Pillars of Wisdom*, and they looked confused. They explained they were studying architecture at a university in Lebanon, but now they were here and they felt isolated. They wrote about the things they missed in Lebanon. They wrote about a special tree and then their mother.

They asked why they couldn't understand some of the things I said. I told them it was because I spoke a regional dialect. I told them I could barely write myself and was by no means an expert.

They asked, "What is this word—dialect?"

I said it's a word like language. It's used for organizing people by class and sometimes ethnicity.

I was joking, but not really. They laughed too, not knowing what I meant.

Then Sabah asked if this was bad? She said, "Should we have you as our teacher then?"

We all laughed. Now *they* were joking.

I said, "To be quite honest, probably not."

Sabah said next time we met she was going to bring me something sweet—something amazing. She was going to bring me a special candy.

Over the next couple of days I imagined what she would bring me. I imagined exotic Lebanese treats. I imagined special candies made with dates or apricots or exotic fruits I'd never tasted before. But when our next meeting came, she reached into her bag and pulled something out. She pulled out a piece of stupid American candy called Laffy Taffy.

It was something exotic all right.

It was something exotic for her.

So I laughed and thanked her. Then later that hour, Alima asked how they could practice their English. I told them not to laugh but I wanted them to watch television and it would probably help them with their English. I told them they could learn how informal English was spoken. I told them I knew they were devout Muslims and were only allowed to speak Arabic in the home, but I asked them to take an hour out each night and try to practice their English by writing to one another and then reading it out loud. I told them the more they grappled with the language, the better off they would be.

But then I stopped.

I told them I didn't want them to give up what was beautiful about their own culture and exchange it for some superficial American culture.

I wanted to protect them.

And I guess I was still trying to protect them that next year when they were in a class I was teaching and this redneck guy just went off and said it. It was my fault for assigning what I assigned. It was a conservative class too, a bunch of foot washing Baptists and rednecks.

It was an essay about terrorism and racial profiling in the post 9-11 environment, but I swear I didn't know he would say it. Our discussion started.

The redneck guy raised his hand. I called on him and he said, "I think if you're a towel head and you're walking around like that—you should expect..."

Towel head?

What the fuck?
The redneck guy kept talking though. I didn't know what to say really. He kept talking about how we needed to confront these people.

He started waving his hands around and repeating, "We need to confront these people."
I said, "Who? These people? Isn't that a sweeping generalization? These people?"
He threw his hands up in the air and said, "What it comes down to is these MUSLIMS need to confront the darker parts of The Koran. I mean they don't think this book is inspired by God, they think this book is God."
So I asked him about Christianity. I asked him how Paul teaches to be a good slave and

then I quoted Jesus: "I come not with an olive branch but with a sword."

So he said that Jews and Christians weren't strapping bombs to themselves and walking into markets.

I noticed in the back Sabah and Alima had their heads down now. A couple of other students in the class were staring at them.

Were they okay?

He just kept going on, "I mean take the Palestinians for instance. This is nothing more than a terrorist organization pretending it's a state."

I said, "O come on now? That's a stereotype. You can't label a whole group of people, a whole nation of people, because of the more radical elements of their society."

Then he said, "That sounds like teacher talk if you ask me."

He said certain stereotypes aren't stereotypes—they have a basis in some sort of truth, that's the reason why stereotypes exist in the first place.

He was angry now. His face was red. He was picking up his books.

He was leaving.

He said his Brother was in the army and getting shot at now because of what these people were doing.

He was almost crying.

He walked to the door. Then he turned and looked at Sabah and Alima and said, "We need to confront these people. We need to confront these terrorists."

He left the room and the door shut behind him.

IT WAS QUIET NOW.

Everyone was looking around. No one was saying anything. I dropped my head and smiled. Others smiled. I took a deep breath and said, "I'm sorry guys."

People nodded their heads and smiled back trying to show me they were sorry this happened in our class too.

I sat with the rest of the class and I tried to explain that sometimes classes get out of hand and I allowed this one to get out of hand without realizing.

I said, "I apologize for anyone who may have been offended."

I breathed deep, "I guess I was wrong in assigning this for today."

I dismissed class for the day and told them I was sorry again. "That's right. Class dismissed."

Now the students left, but a few stuck around to chat.

A quiet student who always came in covered in coal dust walked over and told Alima, "Don't worry about that guy. He's just a jackass. He has more mouth than brains."

Alima looked down and blushed at his word, "Jackass."

Then one of the long skirted Baptist girls came over and said to Alima, "I saw you with your baby the other day. I saw you at the store."

She told Alima she had such a beautiful child. "He really is such a beautiful baby." Then she invited Alima and Sabah to her church picnic on Sunday.

I gathered up my papers and realized I was wrong too in thinking about certain students—

rednecks. What was I thinking? I was a red-neck. I came from rednecks. People laughed at my accent when I travelled anywhere.

So the rest of the students left. Alima and Sabah just sat there. Alima had her head bowed and Sabah was just looking at me with tears in her eyes. They started gathering up their things. They walked to the front of the room. I wanted to tell them again that I was sorry. I wanted to tell them that it was all my fault. I wanted to explain to them that sometimes Socratic class-es like this get out of hand and sometimes it's a good thing, it's a part of learning. They were standing in front of my desk now.

I told them I was sorry, but it was too late now.

It was too late because Sabah was telling me it was Okay.

She said, "I have to deal with it all of the time."

There were tears in her eyes and she said, "It makes me sad. I grew up in Lebanon but I was born in New York. My father worked there for 10 years before we returned home. It makes me sad."

And then the tears turned from sad tears to different tears.

The tears turned into angry tears and Sabah said she understood why people felt that way.

I told her, "I understand why people feel that way but that doesn't mean it's right."

Sabah kept going.

She said, "No, I think you are wrong."

I said, "Why am I wrong then?"

She said, "No, I understand why people feel this way. I really do."

I said, "Why?"

She said, "I understand why people feel this way because…"

And then her eyes flashed full of anger and anguish.

She said, "My people have been tortured and killed and lied about for many years."

But then she stopped.

I said, "What?"

And then she said, "My people."

She stopped again. Then she said, "It's those Jews. It's those filthy Jews."

And now Alima raised her head too and they were saying it together. "It's those Jews. It's those Jews."

Now they were shouting it. They were shouting it except it was more than just an angry shout. It was an angry shout, but now they were smiling.

They were smiling and shouting. "It's the Jews. It really is Mr. McClanahan. It's those Jews."

It had become a chant now and they were saying it together. JEWS. JEWS. JEWS.

It was a song that they were singing and couldn't stop saying, Jews. Jews. Jews.

So I gave up. I bowed my head and gave up. I started smiling too and now I was whispering inside my head. It's the Jews. It's the Jews. It's the Jews.

But STOP.

THERE IS A SECOND ENDING TO TERRORISTS

A COUPLE OF MONTHS LATER I wanted some Chick-Fil-A. So I drove out to the Crossroads Mall and walked inside the mall. I was just about to the fast food joint when I saw them. They were walking down the mall and they looked different somehow. They were still wearing their head scarves, but they were in different outfits. They were wearing tight jeans. I looked down at their feet and they weren't wearing sandals anymore. They were wearing high heels.

And the toes. The toes were painted pink and pedicured.

Their faces looked beautiful.

They were wearing make-up.

Alima had something else now too. She had her son.

He was three or so and he was talking. He was holding a stuffed animal and saying, "Cartoons. Cartoons."

They smiled and waved and walked over. Sabah asked how I was doing. I told them I was fine. I smiled at the boy. Then Sabah told me she was sorry about the way she had behaved in class a few months earlier. I had always been kind to her, but she told me she was sorry. She told me she didn't feel that way now. She didn't know what she felt anymore.

I told her not to worry. The little boy kept shouting about cartoons.

Alima smiled and told me she didn't know what her son was talking about anymore.

I smiled.

She said, "He's an American. He says American things now."

I just kept smiling but I didn't know why.

"My own child is lost to me," she said.

But she didn't look sad.

She looked joyous.

So I bowed my head and said, "Well it was good seeing you."

And so we went our separate ways. I felt sorry somehow and so I turned back around and watched them walk away. I watched them walk away covered in shopping bags. They had on high heeled shoes. They had on tight jeans. They were different now.

Alima was right.

They were all different.

They didn't know what they felt anymore.

They were like all of us.

They were Americans.

A CHAPTER FROM A BOOK I WILL START WRITING IN 2012

ONE NIGHT SARAH CAME HOME and told me about what happened at the hospital that day.

She sat down and ate her fast food from Wendy's, and I listened to her tell me about this twenty year old guy who weighed 520 pounds. The fat kid was admitted because he had something wrong with his breathing.

He kept telling the nurses, "Please let me die. Please let me die."

There were so many things wrong with him they had to fit him with a Foley.

Sarah went into his room and smiled and said, "Okay, we're going to have to put in your catheter now."

The fat kid asked her all nervous, "What's

that?"

Sarah explained it to him. She told him how it went through his penis and how it would empty out all of the urine from his bladder because they didn't want him exerting himself— even if he was only urinating. She knew the guy was nervous.

He looked up at her with his scared eyes and said, "Well okay. But I guess I should tell you something. I guess I should warn you." Sarah said, "What?"

He hesitated and said, "Well, it's real small. My privates. They're real small."

"O don't you worry about that any," Sarah said. "We've seen about everything in here. You've got nothing to be embarrassed about."

She patted him on the back and said, "Part of it is probably your weight. I'm sure you're normal size. Besides that, they have you on that weight program now. They say every five to ten pounds you lose, you gain an inch in penis size. At least that's what they say."

The fat kid didn't laugh.

Sarah took the catheter and bent down. The young man sat at the edge of the bed.

She started pushing past the mounds of flesh, searching for his penis. She pushed some of the flesh away here and then she pushed some of the flesh away there.

But she couldn't find it.

She kept looking.

The fat kid whispered, "O god this is embarrassing."

"Now don't you worry, we've done this before," Sarah repeated. "There's nothing we haven't seen in here."

She kept pushing away the mounds of flab, but she couldn't find it.

Her arms were getting tired.

She stopped for a minute.

She breathed deep.

"I told you it was small," the fat kid said. He was sobbing now.

"I told you my privates were small."

Sarah stood up and patted him on the back, "It's okay."

Then she knelt back down and started trying to find it one last time.

She took all of the strength she had left and pushed back the flesh from the legs. She gagged from the smell.

The fat kid started sobbing, and then Sarah finally found it.

It was just a little nub of flesh. What?

He didn't have any testicles or a penis, only a nub of skin and an opening where he could urinate.

She touched the nub of skin.

The fat kid was whispering and sobbing, "Please let me die. Please."

Sarah didn't say anything but just pushed back the nub of flesh with her finger.

AND THEN:

There was a strip of lint and dirt inside. It had been lodged inside the nub.

And now it falling.

It was falling from the nub so soft and slow, drifting back and forth like a feather. It was falling like a feather falls from an angel wing.

Then fat kid whispered, "Please let me die. Please."

Then the wind picked up the dirt feather and blew it once again into the air. It danced and sparkled and shined in the light.

Sarah said it made her think of one word. It made her think of the word, "Beautiful."

SEX TAPES

I DIDN'T EVEN WANT to watch his sex tape really, but he showed it to me anyway. Shit, I just thought he was joking that day, until he slipped it into the VCR and pushed play.

I couldn't even tell what it was at first, but then I saw a shaky camera and I then I heard Ian telling the woman on the tape, "Don't worry. I'm not gonna show your face. I promise."

And that's when it started.

"I don't know if we should be watching this," I said. "I don't think it's right."

Ian just laughed and told me to shut-up.

"Yeah shut up McClanahan," T.J. said and then they both started laughing together.

Ian fast forwarded the tape and then he stopped.

It was a naked girl.

Holy shit.

It was a naked girl and you couldn't see her face. Ian was laughing.

"Who the hell is she?" T.J. said.

Ian kept hitting the mute button.

"It's a girl I met a couple of weeks ago," Ian said. Then he whispered, "Kinky. Kinky. Kinky."

Then there was a razor and shaving lotion now. She was putting the shaving lotion on and now she was shaving her pubic hair and Ian was laughing. She shaved a couple of strokes and then she took the razor and washed it in a cup of water.

I kept watching. It was a naked woman. Holy shit. It was the body of a naked woman.

So I took my hand and covered my eyes in embarrassment, but now Ian was laughing at me. T.J. punched me in the shoulder and laughed and now I was laughing too.

"What the hell are you so uptight for," Ian said. "It was her idea."

I shook my head and told them that I wasn't

an expert in human nature or anything, but I was sure she didn't want Ian showing it to his friends.

Ian hit pause and said, "Well why would somebody make something like this if there wasn't some danger in other people seeing it? It's the possibility of others seeing it that makes it worth doing in the first place."

I told him he was wrong.

I kept watching it.

Of course, I didn't dare talk about it later with Mandy. Mandy was this girl I liked at work but who always seemed to have a boyfriend. I didn't dare tell her about the tape because I knew she wouldn't approve. That day at lunch, I asked her if she ever got sick of her life, if she ever got sick of her stupid friends.

I told her I was sick of all the fucked up shit my friends did. She sat and listened and then we heard this horrible screeching. It was this tree we always took our breaks by, which was always full of birds for some reason. There were always hundreds of birds in this tree screeching and squawking and screeching some more.

We both laughed at our bird tree and then I said, "Watch this."

What?

I took off running straight at the tree and started kicking the shit out of it. There were all kinds of people around, but I didn't care.

I kicked and kicked and then swoosh—hundreds of birds started flying out from the tree—hundreds of birds all flying from the tree like rockets taking off—and then Mandy started cracking up. I walked back smiling a shit eating grin. The people who were walking by looked at me strange like, "Why would a grown man decide to go kick a tree full of birds?"

"You're crazy," she said and giggled some more.

Then Mandy was quiet.

So I tried changing the subject, "How's your boy doing?"

"My boy," she said. She didn't say anything for a second and then, "Well my boyfriend is no longer my boyfriend. My boyfriend is someone else's boy now."

Then Mandy was quiet again.

I didn't know what to say.

She said, "You think you know people sometimes, but I guess you don't."

✳

So I grinned and told her that I should say I was sorry for her misfortune, but I wasn't that sorry.

"What?" she said and looked confused.

I said, "This is perfect for me."

Then Mandy smiled a smile and asked me why it was perfect.

I said it was perfect because this meant there was going to be some heavy flirting going on.

She giggled again.

I was making her laugh.

I asked her if she wanted to go putt putt golfing with me that weekend.

She said yes.

I told her I was the fucking king of putt putt golf and she would fall in love with me once she saw my mad putt putt golfing skills. If the golfing went well, I'd take her to see some pro-wrestling at the end of the month.

But then the next night I was back at Ian's for some reason and we were shit faced drunk, watching TV with our friend Ashley the Feminist.

Ashley the Feminist said something like, "Let's watch something. I'm bored."

I thought, "O shit no. No."

So Ian turned the VCR on and hit play. The tape was already in the VCR except this was a part I'd never seen before.

"You're fucking joking?" Ashley the Feminist said.

Her mouth was wide open.

Then Ashley the Feminist had a look on her face just like she always did before she started on one of her tirades. "After hundreds of years of trying for something as women, as a minority—this is what we fucking get. We get women sold back to women as porno pop culture, and a promise not to show our faces for some asshole. It's so sad."

She smoked her cigarette.

Ian wasn't sad and started talking to me, "You know after you and T.J. left the other day—he came back and asked if he could come borrow one of my tapes. Get this: he wanted to watch it with his girlfriend. He left me a message this morning when he dropped it off saying, 'My girlfriend liked it.'"

Ashley the Feminist rolled her eyes some more and said, "That's disgusting and this is disgusting. It makes me want to vomit."

Ian pushed pause. "What are you telling me? Just because she's doing this—she's degrading herself. You don't even know her, but I get it. I know how you are. Throw another woman under the bus and start blaming."

Ashley the Feminist was pissed now and said she didn't blame the woman.

She blamed Ian for being such a dickhead.

Then they argued back and forth and I listened to the tape. I couldn't hear the girl on the tape because the volume was so low, but I could hear Ian's voice.

I could hear Ian on the tape saying, "You look so fucking beautiful."

I could hear Ian on the tape saying, "You look so fucking good."

I could hear Ian on the tape saying, "O god, I love you right now."

I finally stood up and stretched,

"Where are you going?" Ashley the Feminist asked.

I told them I needed to go to sleep.

I told them I was going on a putt putt golf date the next day and I needed to be ready.

So I went on my date. I took Mandy putt putt golfing and we shared a 40 ounce and we ate hot dogs. For some reason I couldn't stop thinking about Ian's voice and what he was saying to the headless girl. I tried not to think about it. I guess I was nervous on the date because I started telling inappropriate stories. I told Mandy about how I helped my friends steal cable a couple of nights before. I told her if she wanted free cable I knew how to do it. I'd steal cable for her.

She said, "How romantic."

Then I told her another one of my dumbass stories. I told her how soda machines are unable to recognize the paper quality of dollar bills. They just recognize the image. I told her my friend and I xeroxed a bunch of dollar bills and put them in pop machines.

I said, "I haven't paid for a soda in over three years."

Mandy shook her head and told me that maybe it was a good thing I'd decided to start a new life and quit hanging out with my loser friends.

I shook my head yes. She didn't even know.

Then she said she would like to meet them.

I told her she wouldn't like them. They weren't the type of people to like.

Mandy said, "Do you think I'm judgmental?"

She hit her putt putt golf ball.

Then she said it sounded like I was the one who was judgmental.

I told her it was weird being out with someone from work.

Mandy said, "Yeah it's sad the way we compartmentalize each other."

I agreed.

I hit my putt putt ball and said, "Good god. This conversation is getting serious."

So we played our putt putt.

I told her I liked her.

She told me she liked me too or at least the part she knew about me.

So I felt good. I felt good that night knowing I had someone and could stop hanging out with the people I was hanging out with. I was feeling so good I wanted to stop by and tell Ian, and T.J., and Ashley. I felt like I had someone now and I wasn't going to help with schemes to steal cable or smoke pot at ten in the morning or hang out and watch faceless people fuck. I was free of all that now.

I stopped by that evening and they were already lit. They were all drinking out of these tall plastic glasses full of brandy and they were watching the sex tape.

No one paid any attention to me.

Ashley the Feminist just kept shaking her head at the tape and saying, "This is disgusting."

"Then why did you want to watch it then?" Ian said.

I didn't say anything, but then the camera started shaking.

"O shit this is the part where I was drunk," Ian said and tried to press pause so we couldn't see the woman's face, but it wouldn't pause.

He tried to push pause but it was still playing.

I saw a stomach and then I saw ribs.

I saw a chest and breasts and then... I saw a face.

I saw the face of the girl I knew.

I saw my friend Mandy's face.

Mandy.

It was her.

Then Ian said on the tape, "Oops I'm sorry, I didn't mean to show your face."

Then Ian in real life said, "Well anyway, I guess you know what she looks like now. Some girl who broke up with her boyfriend." The camera panned back up and away from her face. I didn't say anything.

Ashley the Feminist said, "She's really beautiful. Let me see her face again. Let me see."

Ian laughed, "No, no."

But then he did. He hit rewind. I saw her face, breasts, ribs, stomach and thighs.

Then he hit play.

I saw thighs.

I saw stomach.

I saw ribs.

I saw breasts.

Then I saw her face.

Mandy.

The girl from work.

And then I saw something else.

I saw that the whole world was one shitty coincidence after another. I saw someone rolling their eyes at chance—O god that's ridiculous. I saw how I wanted to believe in order too. I wanted to believe in the mundane shit of the world. But now I saw that the world was stupid chance.

*

So I didn't even say anything else to them. I didn't tell them that just a few minutes before I thought my life was changing. I didn't ask Ian how he knew my friend. I didn't tell them anything. I walked outside and vomited on my way home. I left and didn't go to bed that night wondering what I was going to do.

The next morning at dawn I was back at Ian's apartment. The sun was rising. So I knocked and it took fifteen minutes before anyone came to the door.

I won't tell you what I asked.

I won't tell you what he said, but I will tell you this. I left his apartment that morning with the sex tape stuffed beneath my shirt. I went back to my apartment and watched it alone.

I wanted to watch it. I wanted to watch Mandy.

And watch it—I did. I watched it that morning and then I watched it an hour later and then an hour later and then an hour after that. I didn't leave my apartment for the rest of the day. I hardly left my apartment for a week and then two weeks. I noticed the flashing messages on my phone and pushed play. One message was from my job telling me I didn't have a job anymore. The other one was from Mandy. She said she had a really great time last week, but she was worried. She wondered where I was. She didn't know what was wrong with me.

I didn't call her back though. I didn't need her now. I knew I didn't need anyone.

Over the next couple of weeks the phone just kept ringing. The phone rang and rang. I sat in the room watching the video. I watched the video over and over again. I turned up the volume real loud so I could hear the voices, but I could still barely hear them. I could hear Ian talking but I couldn't hear Mandy talking.

I could hear Ian saying, "O you look so fucking beautiful."

So I turned it up.

She said in a whisper, "I love you."

Ian said, "You look so fucking good."

She said in a whisper, "I love you."

So I pushed rewind. The tape went past everything—the chest, the breasts, the thighs, the thighs, the feet. Then I pushed play.

I hit mute.

I said, "You look so beautiful."

I clicked the mute off.

She said, "I love you."

I pretended she said "I love you" to me.

I hit mute. I said what Ian said, "O God I want you so bad."

I turned the mute off.

She said, "I love you."

The phone was ringing now. I didn't have any clothes on anymore. I let it play. I didn't answer the phone. I pushed mute.

I said, "I love you."

I turned the mute off.

She said, "I love you."

I said...

And so I sat and watched some more, but soon I started looking away and when I looked back it was all different now.

I still saw legs.

I still saw feet.

I saw thighs.

I saw stomach.

I saw chest but there was something different now. The feet were my feet. The thighs were my thighs. The sex was my sex, but her sex too, the sex of us both. The stomach was my stomach. The chest was my chest. So now Ian's camera panned up and I saw that the face was my face and now I was turning up the volume with one hand. I saw that I was saying to my-self, "You look so fucking good."

I turned it up but I could barely hear my own voice on the other line saying, "I love you Scott."

Now I was saying this to myself in real life, "You look so beautiful Scott."

I turned it up and I heard what sounded like my own voice on the tape. I love you.

I saw at last the true nature of sex.

I saw myself saying, "I love you Scott."
I love you.
And Scott said, "I love you too Scott."
I love you too.
I love you Scott.
I love you.
I love you.

BUT THERE IS A SECOND ENDING TO SEX TAPES TOO

Ten years later I was sitting around the house one evening when the phone rang.

It was T.J. and he said, "What was Ian's first name?"

"What," I said.

"What was Ian's real first name that he didn't go by?"

"What the fuck are you talking about?"

I thought for a moment.

I said, "Merle."

"What year was Ian born?"

I felt worried. I thought for a second and said, "I think 1976." I heard T.J. counting in his head. Then he said. It's him.

He read: "A man identified as Merle Anderson, 36, died from multiple gunshot wounds late Saturday night along with a female companion."

I put the phone down.

It was him.

I went to the wake the next night. That morning in the paper I found out he'd brought a girl home at one in the morning. The girl's ex-boyfriend was waiting in the bushes outside her apartment. As soon as Ian stopped his truck, the ex-boyfriend walked out and fired.

Then he fired again.

Then he did it again.

Then he did it again.

He emptied a whole clip from the glock into Ian's body. Then the ex-boyfriend switched clips.

The girl ran around screaming, "What are you doing? You killed him."

He took the glock, pointed it at her head and shot her in the face. The ex-boyfriend shot the girl in the face until her face wasn't her face anymore. Then the ex-boyfriend went to his Mom and Dad's house and went to sleep in a bed with cartoon sheets.

Ian didn't make it.

✳

I stayed at the wake for about fifteen minutes before I left. I heard Ian's brother talking about how he saw Ian's body. He said he wished he wouldn't have asked to see it. He said it didn't look like the way a dead body should look.

Ian's brother said, "Holes. He was full of holes."

On the way out I saw a woman with children and an overweight husband. The husband was sweaty and chasing after her. I smiled at the man. She passed by. She smiled back at me and then I saw her face.

It was her face. It was Mandy's face?

Was it?

So I mean this now. This story is worthless, especially stories that aren't telling stories. All stories told by a man with a woman in it are always about the men who are telling it. So I won't leave you with a story. I'll leave you with a letter—a letter written to ghosts. I am writing to the ghost of my friend Ian Anderson, or maybe I'm writing to my own ghost because all stories about ghosts are always about the ghost who is writing them.

So I am writing to the ghost of us.

I am writing a set of directions.

Travel on Interstate 64 to Beckley WV.

Taker the Harper Road exit and turn right.

Take a left at the gas station on Pikeview Drive.

Take that road past the Chinese place.

Take a left at the top of the hill past the apartments. Take another left at Teel and then take a right on Rider. I'm in the 5th house on the left. Do it now before it's too late ghosts.

I will be waiting.

AND NOW A NOTE ON LITERARY REVERENCE

FUCK YOU JAMES JOYCE, Sam Beckett, and all the rest of them.

It's year zero.

SO NOW A LIST OF THINGS I'M ASHAMED OF

1. I'M ASHAMED of some things I did when I was a kid.

2. I'm ashamed of the time I yelled at my father at Christmas.

3. I'm ashamed of when the girls pulled my pants down in the 7th grade and my penis was tiny.

4. I'm ashamed of the time I drove a U-HAUL into the side of a gas station.

5. I'm ashamed of the time I hit my house with my car.

6. I'm ashamed of how I treated my Uncle Grover the last time I saw him.

7. And I'm ashamed of what I did to Nicky.

NICKY

Nicky was a year younger than me, 15, and he used to ride his motorcycle up behind my house and go mossing. In the evening he left with his motorcycle weighed down by green moss, which he took into town and sold for $30. I remember seeing him ride when I was shooting basketball in the evenings and the girls on the road sat around and watched me. The girls were in junior high and smoked cigarettes.

One day Nicky stopped his dirt bike and started shooting hoops. He was friendly and the girls were laughing at everything he said.

Nicky and I played a pick up game and he started beating my ass. He shot a jumper from the corner and he made it. He stole the ball from me when I tried to crossover dribble. He pounded it down inside and pushed me out of the way. He dunked the basketball—two handed.

Then I saw something, the girls weren't watching me anymore.

They were watching Nicky. He shook my hand and smiled and then he hopped up on his dirt bike. He jump-started it, waved, and drove off.

The next couple of days—it was all about Nicky.

"Nicky is so funny."

"Nicky rides a motorcycle."

"Nicky makes $150 dollars on moss each week, and he uses the money to take care of his Mom and pay their rent. She's real bad to drink."

One day the girls stopped coming to watch me shoot ball. I went outside that evening like always but they were all down by the pile of timber. They were all standing around, and the girl I liked most of all, Cindy, was sitting on Nicky's lap. She had her arm around his neck and his hands were in places my hand used to be. I walked into the woods and snuck up behind them to hear what they were talking about. It was dark by now so they couldn't see me.

I listened.

Cindy, the girl I liked best was making fun of me.

She said, "His teeth are so big."

So I sat and listened and watched her kiss him.

I knew I had to get rid of Nicky.

There weren't many opportunities though. He always parked his motorcycle in front of the Anger's Doberman that barked and shat and dug big ass holes. But then one day I got my chance. One day he ended up parking his dirt bike in the alley behind the Anger's woodpile and he went inside. I walked by and listened to Nicky and the girls laughing inside the house. There was smoke coming out of the open windows and love sounds. I knelt behind the woodpile and listened. I was always too shy and afraid about getting them pregnant. Nicky didn't care. I imagined myself cool enough for all the girls to stand around and laugh when I told stories and punch me in the arm and then smile. I wished I wasn't so skinny. Then there were cries of love.

＊

I looked at the beat up motorcycle.

I STOLE IT.

I stood the bike up, and kicked the kick stand from beneath it. I didn't start it, but I took off running with it to the top of the dirt pile. The dirt pile was this giant mound of dirt and rocks where the timber company had cleared off the land from behind our houses. It was a field of nothing but briars and sandstone chunks full of fossils, broken up rocks and deep ditches. At the top of the pile right next to the side of the mountain were all of these locust trees with black berry bushes growing up around them. I ran with the motorcycle and jumped the ditches. I bounced the dirt bike tire over the rocks—bounce, bounce. I ran right up to the thicket and dropped the dirt bike down into the weeds where it disappeared. Then I walked away wondering if anyone saw me.

I thought, "O shit."

I went inside my house and waited. An hour passed and it was getting dark. I waited and then I watched Nicky walking back down the alley like he was looking for something. He would never find it in those bushes. The girls were looking for the motorcycle too.

I thought, "Why did I do that?"

That night I lay awake thinking, "I should tell someone. No. I should go get the motorcycle from the weeds and just put it back behind the house where he left it."

But I didn't. I just sat and let my mind wander with all the possible ways I could be caught...

"Did the Angers see me taking the bike and running with it?"

"Did Mrs. Baker see me running up to the dirt pile with it?"

Her husband was dying of cancer in the back bedroom of the double wide. The windows were always opened and I heard him dying. At night you could hear him moaning.

"If Mrs. Baker was in that back bedroom she could have watched me do it."

I thought they knew what had happened and they were just waiting to use it against me. "Should I try going back to the locust trees and try digging it out of the weeds?"

"Should I?"

It was too risky.

＊

So I went to church the next morning. Instead of sitting in the back with my friend Mike and raising hell, I stayed away. All Mike ever did was rip out his pubes when you weren't looking and then drop a few of the short and curlies on your arm just to be an asshole.

I didn't need any of that this morning. I needed to pray. I didn't pray for forgiveness though.

I prayed, "Dear father in heaven, please keep me from getting caught."

I was still praying a few hours later when I went back home and started shooting baskets at the end of the alley.

I took a shot and I prayed.

I took a shot and I prayed.

Then I saw this cop car rolling up our gravel road. I made sure my back was turned so they wouldn't see my face. I kept shooting hoops.

They rolled past me and then around the block—once, twice, and then three times.

Then they left.

I kept shooting basketball and wondered if they knew. The next day I walked down the block past the continentals and listened to Thelma talking about what was going on. She was sitting on the porch with Mrs. Baker and they were smoking cigarettes and reading soap opera magazines. Somebody brought up the stolen motorcycle. I didn't say anything for a second but tried to act surprised.

I said, "What?" like I didn't know what was going on. Mrs. Baker flipped through the soap opera magazine and she started talking about something else.

They didn't know it was me.

I walked back home dribbling my basketball and I felt some peace, "Did I just get away with it? Did I really get away with it?"

That night I prayed again. I prayed to keep me safe. I knew there were moments one met that started you on a different path.

Was this mine?

Was there a possibility of turning left that would lead to some strange future?

Was there a particular choice that set off a series of events that were beyond my control? It was only a stupid motorcycle, but would it lead me to disaster one day?

*

A day passed and then another and then another and there was no sign of Nicky. There
wasn't even talk of the stolen dirt bike anymore.
It didn't bother me. The girls were back watching me shoot hoops in the evenings. I held
them close afterwards and felt things moving.

Then one night after sundown, we saw this
strange looking woman walking up the street.
She had dyed blonde hair and a little tank top.
She was wobbling back and forth coming closer to us.

Sissy said, "I don't think that woman's
wearing a bra."

You could almost see a breast HANGING
OUT. She came closer and kept wobbling.
Then Sissy said, "I think that woman's shit
faced."

There was someone else walking behind
her.

It was Nicky. Nicky was following behind her,
except he looked like he was hurt. He was all
bent over and the closer he came—we could
see he was covering his face.

Cindy said, "What's up with his face?"

He was walking closer. He was walking fast. His face was bloody and bruised. He was trying to catch up to his mother.

"Mommy," he shouted behind her until she stopped. I stood dribbling the basketball and the girls were watching them argue.

Nicky was telling his mother, "I looked for it. Honestly, I looked."

"You didn't look," she shouted. "We're totally fucked now."

And then we saw her hit him. She just reared back and knocked the shit out of him. Her fist popped against his jaw. Nicky stood still. She hit him again. He fell to the ground. Cindy and Sissy squealed like little mice.

I kept dribbling my basketball and said, "You better not go down there girls."

Nicky put his hands in front of his face like he was praying. He was praying except the prayer was a prayer of blood.

And then it was quiet.

And then he was crying. And then his mother was slapping him against the head.

She had her keys in her hand and she was hitting him now. He was crying. She was screaming at him for losing the motorcycle.

He was trying to get away. "No Mommy."

He was almost a grown man, but he was saying, "No Mommy."

Then he said, "I didn't lose it. Somebody stole it. I promise someone stole it."

He was a five year old boy now and we were watching him.

His mother took one of her keys and tried stabbing him in the neck. Then she was gone. Nicky followed her and kept crying. I dribbled my basketball. The girls did nothing.

I never saw Nicky again. But I heard stories.

These were stories told by old friends. Nicky couldn't moss anymore because the motorcycle was gone. Nicky's Mom moved away with her boyfriend. Nicky started living in a tent because he couldn't afford the rent at the welfare apartments. He went mossing one day to get some money, but since he didn't have the bike he had to carry the moss himself. He ended up twisting his knee coming down off the mountain and he couldn't play basketball anymore. He started wandering the streets of Rainelle where he met this older girl. She was the one who showed him how to huff. One night after they got into a fight he sprayed a plastic bag full of cooking spray and then he put the plastic bag over his head. He breathed deep. He died.

*

So I don't know what made me do it. It had been five years at least. My life had been going well since then and I'd even moved away. It was like I was living with a special power inside me. One night I found myself driving around town. My buddy C.W. was dating a girl who lived on the street where I used to live. The girl's mom was gone and he wanted to fuck the girl. I dropped him off at the welfare apartments. I walked around the old continentals. I walked up the road cut by the logging company. I walked back to the dirt pile and the tuft of old locust trees.

I thought about Nicky again and it was like he was here. I walked closer and looked into the weeds and…

The motorcycle was still there.

"What the hell?"

It was just sitting in the thick weeds.

I thought the dirt bike would have been gone by now. I thought someone would have found it after all of this time.

It was just like I'd left it though. The girls we once knew had their own babies now. They were fat girls by now smoking cigarettes and reading soap opera magazines. I thought about judgment day and then I picked up the dirt bike. I thought about all of the moments of our lives and the events created by single moments. I walked with the dirt bike and I hopped on it and I decided to ride. I kick started it just for fun.

It started. What the fuck? I felt like I should cry at this strange miracle, five year old gasoline starting a motorcycle, but I didn't cry. I found myself doing something else. I found myself laughing like some triumphant God. I found myself laughing a laugh just like I'm laughing now.

I found myself laughing,

HAH HAH HAH

HAH...HAH..........HAH

HAH

Can you hear me?

NOW SOME PUBLIC APOLOGIES

I WOULD LIKE to publicly apologize to Christy Ford who stopped speaking to me after I got inebriated and shouted at some anti-war protesters in 2004. I actually agreed with them politically, but I was just trying to be funny. You were obviously not amused. However, if you do not accept my apology, I would like back the CDs you borrowed.

I would also like to apologize to anyone who recently purchased and did not like *Stories V!* If this is the case, please abstain from writing about it on your personal blog. You are not the *New York Times* and I'm not (insert famous writer here). I will take your silence as announcement enough of your dislike.

I would also like to apologize for placing curses on those who wrote negatively about my books in the past. As of today, I have officially lifted those curses. This does not include those writers with the initials PC and CDW. May the pox on your houses continue!

LOVE LETTERS

O BUT ENOUGH with sad stories. Who told you there is no such thing as real, true, and eternal love? Cut out the lying tongue of the fucker.

Follow me now dear reader, and only me, and I will show you the story of a heart. I will show you the story of a heart with a name written inside it.

Sarah,

This isn't the cheapo $5 bouquet either. This is the real deal $10 one. Please love me. I'll make it worth your while in the long run.

Bubbies

12-4-04

RAZY

I HAD THIS CAT named Iggy who had sexual problems. If you touched his whiskers or even walked a little too close to him, he'd start having a panic attack.

He'd start gagging—gah.

Gah.

And then he'd gag some more. And then he'd try to hump your leg.

Then I had this dog named Buddy who really wasn't our dog even but was just this hobo dog who showed up at our house one day all friendly and happy. He used to show up and stay with us for years at a time and then take off and go travelling. The last time I saw him he was hitchhiking on Sewell Mountain. A semi stopped and he got inside the truck. He was on his way to California.

But then there was Razy.

Of course, I don't even know why he did it really. One day we looked up and Razy was gone. I know it hadn't been that long since February. That night I was in bed not even thinking about Razy. My Dad was getting ready to go to work. Razy was an outside cat, and since it was cold, Razy was up inside of our long ass Oldsmobile, next to the engine, trying to keep warm. My Dad went outside to start the engine and warm the car up. And when he did, all we heard were these O shit screams, and then a high pitched yelp like eeeeeeeeeee. Even though I was inside the house trying to sleep—it startled me awake from my thoughts of Mary Ann Elmore.

My Mom and I ran to the door.

She said, "What's happening Gary? What happened?"

The car was still running with exhaust popping out the back. Pop. Pop. Pop.

There were these big wads of fur everywhere and there was blood, and a trail of blood.

And there was a cat tail curling and twirling like a snake in the snow.

The fan belt must have cut it off.

My Dad took the flashlight and followed the specks of blood until he found Razy beneath bushes and the broken cinder blocks, shaking and crying and crying and shaking....

But he lived.

That night my Mom wrapped an old t-shirt around Razy's tail stump. The next day we buried the cat tail in the backyard. We visited the tail grave the next week and mourned. My Mom saved what was left of Razy's tail by putting a rubber band around his stump.

That seemed to stop the bleeding for awhile.

And since we didn't have a vet closer than two hours away, she called him the next morning and they told her to put the tail stub in tin foil.

That's what she did.

So Razy started getting better. His balance was horrible now, but it was more than that. It was like he was changed somehow.

It wasn't like he was mean or anything. It was just that he was tougher than shit and he was always getting into fights. There were these two Doberman pinchers who lived next door and dug holes in the ground deep enough to bury a baby inside. They belonged to this guy who rode in a motorcycle gang called Brothers of the Wheel. One evening when the guy was out riding—the Dobermans broke loose and surrounded Razy. I tried shooing them away, but Mom just pulled me back.

Then all of the sudden Razy spun around with his flying claws and jumped and hopped and scratched and bit. It was like he had something to show us now. It was like he was somehow repaying the world for the lost tail. So we stood and watched the Dobermans run back to their yard yelping and bleeding in pain.

Then a couple of days later my Dad came home talking about Walter Brown in middle town, and how Walter was talking about how many cats there were around his house, and how many mean ass tomcats there were, fighting over who was going to get the females. Walter said if Rainelle had a dog catcher, he'd call him. My Mom said we should probably think about getting Razy fixed, especially since he was fighting so much and getting ready to go catting around.

Even though I was a little boy I knew what "catting around" meant.

Razy listened to all of this sitting on his butt in the La-Z-Boy.

Of course, Razy never sat around like he was a regular cat. He always sat on his butt, sitting up just like he was a real person, almost like the loss of his tail meant that he wasn't a cat anymore.

So if he wasn't a cat anymore, what was he?

❋

The next morning when we woke up, he was gone. Even when we came home from school that afternoon, he didn't come running to say "hi" like he usually did. He was just gone.

Mom put out his food the next day.

Then she put out his food the day after.

She did it the day after that.

Then she did it the day after that.

But the food was always still there the next morning, except for one time when a possum came by and ate it.

After a week we were starting to wonder. We were wondering if he was ever coming back. We all got in my Dad's truck and rolled down the windows and drove around Rainelle shouting, "Razy." We talked about how we brought him home from Grandma Ruby's just a few years before with his little brother named Blackie and how Blackie was sick, but how Razy kept climbing out of the box on the way back.

On the way back home I said all excited, in my little boy voice, "Mom he's getting out of the box again. He's getting out."

Then Razy's little brother Blackie died.

But Razy lived.

So we shouted "Razy," but we couldn't find him.

We thought he was gone.

But then one day, a month or so later, Dad came back home and said he talked to Walter Brown. You wouldn't believe it. Walter said there was this tail-less cat running around middle town fighting every tomcat over there. He said the tail less cat took on four cats one day and then he took on three the next. He said they were fighting so much there was blood in front of the welfare apartments. He said how his daughter Heather had pulled the tail-less cat off another tom because she thought Razy was going to kill it. He said there was a look of death inside the tail-less cat's eyes. He said he wondered if this cat was Razy.

That evening we drove over to the welfare apartments and we started shouting "Razy" again.

Then we drove a little more.

"Razy! Razy!"

And then all of a sudden here came Razy. His front paw was bloody and gnawed looking and he was hopping on three legs like the other leg was hurt. He had to keep stopping and resting like his back was broken. He couldn't control his bowels anymore

Stop.

Run.

Stop.

Crap.

Run.

Stop.

Run.

One of his eyes was swollen shut and we thought it had been gouged out. My Mom pursed her lips like she always did when she was worried. Then she had a look on her face like she was getting ready to cry. There was a piece of his left ear missing and it had been replaced by a bloody scab.

Razy just kept hobbling over to us though like he was saying, "Don't leave me... please don't leave me... I'm coming... I'm slow, but I'm coming."

And so he stepped into the truck and whined a little about the hurt. I kissed his head and held him in my lap and he sat and purred so soft.

Razy was our cat again.

Later in the year my Mom woke me up one night. It was late summer and we could hear something outside.

I said, "Mom? What is it?"

She said, "Well why don't you come and see."

I walked into the kitchen and I could hear something. I could hear the sounds of Razy's bowl going tinkle tinkle tinkle against the concrete porch outside.

＊

My Mom lifted me up and turned on the porch light and it shined so bright in the backyard.

What did I see?

I saw at least 40—50?—60?—70? kittens at our back porch eating Razy's food.

I saw Razy standing among them like a proud father.

My Mom said, "That's unusual. Usually the tomcat tries to kill the kittens so he can have the mommy to himself again."

"But not Razy," I said.

"But not Razy," she said.

So Razy sat among them making sure they took their turns at his bowl. He was licking their foreheads clean. Over in the background, beside the outbuildings were all of the Mommy cats watching the babies eat, 5, 6, 7, 8, 9, 10 Mommy cats.

And Razy was letting the kittens eat all of his food too and he was just sitting there because he was their daddy. He was their Daddy

all right, staring at the beauty and balance of
their long, long, Loooooooooooooooooooooooo
ooooooooooooooooooooooooooooooooooooooo
ooooooooooooooooooooooooooooooooooooooo
ooooooooooooooooooooooooooooooooooooooo
ooooooooooooooooooooooooooooooooooooooo
ooooooooooooooooooooooooooooooooooooooo
ooooooooooooooooooooooooooooooooooooooo
ooooooooooooooooooooooooooooooooooooooo
ooooooooooooooooooooooooooooooooooooooo
ooooooooooooooooooooooooooooooooooooooo
ooooooooooooooooooooooooooooooooooooooo
ooooooooooooooooooooooooooooooooooooooo
ooooooooooooooooooooooooooooooooooooooo
ooooooooooooooooooooooooooooooooooooooo
ooooooooooooooooooooooooooooooooooooooo
oooooooooooooong
                    tails.

DEAD BABY JOKES

WHAT'S THE DIFFERENCE between a dead baby and a rock?

That's what Billy asked me late that night when he came into the office to pick up something. I wasn't expecting a dead baby joke. He had two women with him. They were in party dresses and they had all been drinking.

He turned to me and said, "Hey McClanahan. You're McClanahan right?"

I nodded my head "Yes."

And that's when he asked me.

I just shook my head "No" at the joke and smiled faintly.

＊

He repeated, "Well the difference between a dead baby and a rock is you can't fuck a rock."

Shit.

What the fuck?
I looked at the women to see whether or not they were going to laugh.

And instead of the women smacking his face or saying they wanted him to take them home immediately, they just twirled their hair and laughed a laugh. Billy looked at me and smiled like he was showing me something about the world. He was showing me something about the way life worked.
I thought, "Who the fuck is this guy?"

＊

Of course, I got the chance to find out just a couple of days later. I was doing this story on a comedian who was touring through town. In the middle of the comedian's act—Billy stopped by.
He was dressed in casual clothes and after

my interview with the comedian, Billy asked me, "Hey you want to go shoot some hoops?"

I said "Yeah" and then he asked me if I could drive.

I just thought we'd stop by some local outdoor court or go to a park somewhere, but as we drove, I realized he was giving me directions to the Coliseum. The Coliseum?

I was confused. I didn't say anything as he took out his keys and unlocked the place. He was a twenty five year old guy with keys to the Coliseum. We walked past the trophies and the retired jersey of Jerry West and then past the offices.

Billy took out his keys again and un-locked the door to one of the coach's office and asked, "Do you want some candy?"

"We probably shouldn't be doing this," I said.

Billy didn't say anything.

There was a stack of autographs of the latest star they gave out to area kids.

"Do you want some free autographed pictures?" He asked me.

I shook my head, "No."

And so we went out onto the court and the

place looked enormous. I asked him how he had keys to the place and he just smiled.

Then he said, "Don't worry about it."

We started shooting and then all of sudden here came the Coach.

The Coach.

This was the guy I saw on television.

The coach was all pissed off and looking at me like I'd broken into the place. "What the hell are you doing in here?"

It was midnight.

I pointed to Billy and suddenly the coach's expression changed.

The coach smiled and said, "O I'm sorry. Hey Billbo. You need anything?"

He waved and repeated, "Can I get you anything Bill?"

Billy shook his head, "No."

He said we were just going to shoot around for awhile.

I thought—who the hell is this guy?

So when Billy called me up two days later and asked if I wanted to go to a restaurant with a couple of the women he knew, I immediately said yes. Then I backtracked after he said the name of the restaurant because I knew I wouldn't be able to afford it. I usually only had five or ten dollars in my pocket or I was figuring it out if I could make rent.

Billy said, "If you're worried about money—then don't. I'm taking care of the check."

I laughed and said, "Okay. I'll go then."

We went to a restaurant that evening and I was still nervous about money. Billy's girl Abby was there and she had a friend with her as well. For some reason they made me feel nervous. They were as skinny as spiders and then one of the women started laughing about the horrible jokes she heard Billy tell.

Billy said, "O you mean what's the difference between a dead baby and a rock?"

He told us the punch line. The women shook their heads and laughed.

"That's so horrible," Abby said. "That's so horrible. I mean it's not even human."

Then Billy told another, "How do you make a four year old boy cry twice?"

We waited.

He said, "Wipe your bloody dick on his teddy bear."

Now the women laughed even harder.

I laughed too even though I didn't know why.

I thought the jokes were disgusting.

The women said, "O Billy, you're so crazy."

Then they kept laughing.

Then they excused themselves and went to the bathroom.

I turned to him and said, "How in the fuck do you get away with saying shit like that?" Billy just smiled and said, "O let's just say it's like a little experiment if you will." He was quiet for a moment and then he said, "You're going to find out people don't care about what the fuck someone is saying, only whether or not they like the person saying it."

He smiled and said, "It's a shallow, shallow, shallow world McClanahan."

Then he was quiet and said, "You know what the most fucked up joke in the world is?" He didn't wait for my answer. "Knock Knock. Who's there?"

I shook my head again.

I didn't understand what he was talking about.

※

So the women came back about that time and sat down. They asked me how long I had been friends with Billy.

Billy said, "A week and a half."

The women laughed again, and then they started talking. It was the kind of talking people do when they excuse themselves to go to the bathroom and come back under the influence of prescription medication. Their eyes were dilated and they looked spacey. Abby told Stephanie she read somewhere that we're all just a collection of other people. "There's no such thing as an individual just a collection of all the people you've ever known. I mean we have so much bacteria inside of us already. We have so many parasites living off of us we don't even know."

Stephanie nodded her head. I didn't know what they were talking about.

Billy just smiled at the women and then he looked at me. He winked.

He was saying, "See."

I was still worried about money.

Billy leaned over and said, "Don't worry about it. I've told you I'm taking care of dinner tonight. Nobody pays their own way in this world. Everything is a lot cheaper than it looks."

Then he reached into his pocket and pulled out the thickest wad of cash I'd ever seen before. There had to have been five thousand dollars there. He smiled again and listened to Abigail's garbled rambling.

And then...

Out of the corner of my eye—I noticed a dark haired woman sitting at the bar. She had black eyes. She was talking with the bartender like she knew him, but she was alone.

I stared at her and then I looked away. Then I started staring again.

She was running her finger against the side of her glass. I watched her and on her wrist there was a tattoo.

What was it? I looked closer. It was the tattoo of a tiny BUTTERFLY.

Billy leaned over and whispered to me, "She's beautiful isn't she? It's a good thing I let you borrow a tie."

I smiled and he said, "Why don't you go talk to her?"

＊

I just laughed at how ridiculous it sounded.

What?

So Billy paid the bill and then he tipped the waiter. The women we were with went outside to smoke.

Billy said, "I'm serious—why don't you go talk to her."

"What?

He said, "I'm telling you to do it."

So Billy went outside too.

They were gone now.

I was alone.

I walked over to the bar and thought about what I could say to the woman with the butterfly tattoo. I didn't want to sound like an asshole.

I said, "I like your tattoo. I have the same one myself."

"Oh you do," she smiled and looked up at me. "Where is it?'

I looked down at my wrists. "Woops I must have forgotten it tonight."

Shit.

I sounded like an asshole.

*

The woman with the butterfly tattoo said, "Well before you get started, I should probably tell you. I'm married."

Then she showed me the ring on her finger.
FUCK.

I turned and smiled and thought, "I can notice a fucking butterfly tattoo but I can't notice a ring."

I walked away. The bartender started laughing at me. I guess this happened all the time to the woman with the butterfly tattoo. He walked over and whispered to a couple of the waiters. And then almost in unison the entire wait staff in the restaurant looked and they were laughing at me. I just kept walking.

I went outside and Billy was waiting. He looked at me.

I just shook my head, "No."

So we walked to the car with the women and then Billy started patting his coat.

"I think I left something inside," he said.

So he left me sitting in the car and waiting with the women. I listened to them chat about what they were going to do the next day.

And then Abigail looked at her watch and

said, "What's he doing in there? It's like he's been gone forever."

They passed their pills around. I said no thank you. He *had* been gone for awhile. It wasn't a couple of minutes later though, Billy came walking that cool walk he always walked with the collar of his trench coat flipped up.

He sat down beside me in the car and we drove away. Abigail and Stephanie were giving him hell about what took him so long. He told them he just couldn't find what he was looking for, but then he smiled and showed me a napkin from the bar.

The women couldn't see it.

It was a napkin that read: Rebecca. 686-0432.

I couldn't believe it. What the fuck?

It must have been the woman with the butterfly tattoo.

And so we went out like this time after time, always with the women. He always paid. I never asked why.

The day after our first evening at the restaurant, he told me all about Rebecca—the woman with the butterfly tattoo. He told me the reason why he took so long in the restaurant. He told me how they started talking and then he followed her to the bathroom. He said that's where it happened.

He said, "And get this. She has a tattoo on her ass too. And you're never going to guess what it is."

He smiled his smile. "It's a caterpillar. The circle of life man. The motherfucking circle of life."

I smiled.

He didn't smile though. He asked me if I was mad at him for taking Rebecca, the woman at the bar. I told him not to worry about it.

But I was jealous.

The woman with the butterfly tattoo had a name. Her name was Rebecca.

I heard all about her from Billy. He said she called him one night when Abigail was over. It scared the shit out of him that Abigail was going to ask who was on the phone. Then the next night he took Rebecca to dinner. They saw Rebecca's husband outside the restaurant waiting on them. The husband chased them at 90 miles an hour through the streets of the city.

They lost him at a park and had sex in her car, wondering if her husband would catch them. He said she was crazy. She was crazy, but he liked her.

Later that same night she took him to an apartment. She said it belonged to her Sister. Her Sister was out of town. They did it on the living room floor. Then Billy said he heard somebody snoring in the other room. He walked down the hallway.

He said it was her husband snoring.

This wasn't her Sister's apartment. This was the apartment she shared with her husband. Rebecca just laughed and flashed her crazy eyes.

Then Billy said he wanted the three of us to go out and eat one night.

He winked at me and said, "Who knows what might happen?"

He smiled, "Rebecca has been talking about you. She said you were cute that night trying to talk to her, but you scare too easy."

It never happened.

✳

It never happened because one day the cops arrested Billy at work. I was walking up the street and I saw the cops putting him in the back of the car. He was in handcuffs and he had his head down. I ran towards them, but they were already gone by the time I got there. The lights flashed and burped and flashed.

I went back home. An hour later my phone rang. It was Abigail. She was hysterical and crying.

"What's going on?" I asked trying to figure it out.

I couldn't hear what Abigail was saying, but then she said, "He's in trouble."

What?

"He's in a lot of trouble Scott."

What?

Billy.

Then Abigail explained, "He was arrested this morning for grand larceny. They're claiming he stole 14,000 dollars from a coach's office in the Coliseum."

I couldn't breathe.

Then she told me his brother was getting ready to bail him out, but he was in serious trouble. She said, "They have video of him taking it too."

Then she stopped again and said, "They have video Scott. They have security videos of Billy taking money and other things too."

That night I called him about two or three times but nobody was answering. I was getting ready for bed when I decided to call him again. It rang. No one was answering. I was getting ready to put the phone down when someone finally picked up.

It was Billy and he was saying, "Hello" in a quiet voice.

"What the hell?" I asked.

He said, "I can't talk that long. I don't want to wake up B."

"B?" I said.

It was like nothing was wrong.

"Who the fuck is B?" I asked. "What the fuck is going on?"

He just giggled and said, "O, I mean Rebecca. B. You know the woman with the tattoo?"

I shook my head.

I said, "Where the fuck is Abby, Billy?"

Billy said, "Who?"

I couldn't believe it.

I said, "Your fucking girlfriend."

Billy was quiet for a moment and then he said, "It's over. She's pretty pissed about what happened."

So I asked again, "What the hell is going on?"

He knew exactly what I was talking about.

He said, "O, now let's not play all innocent. You don't think eating at those restaurants every night on the salary we make is possible do you?"

I breathed deep and waited and then I finally said, "Well what are you going to do?"

He told me he was just going to wait until the trial started, see if his lawyer could get him a deal.

I heard myself repeating dead baby jokes inside my head.

"What's the difference between a dead baby and a rock?"

"How do you make a four year old boy cry twice?"

One day three months later, I stopped by to see him. He gave me directions to this new place where he was working. All the way there I imagined what it would be. I imagined he would be working at an ad agency or a law firm, or picked up another writing gig, but when I pulled up to the address he gave me—I saw what it was.

This was his new job. This was where Billy was working now.

It was a shoe store.

So when I walked inside he looked differ-ent than before. It had only been a couple of months since I last saw him, but now he was unshaven and he had put on weight. His teeth looked whittled down, and he couldn't really talk anyway, because he was so busy waiting on customers.

I stood at the entrance of the store.
Billy looked my way, nodded his head "Hey" and then he came over and asked for me to wait a second. He went over to his boss and asked her if he could take a break. I watched the boss shake her head, "No." She pointed to her watch and gave him a look. Billy smiled and tried to convince her again.

She pointed to her watch and said, "You get off in an hour. How about taking a break then?"

Then she pointed to the people in the store, "I have a whole store full of customers here. Can't you see?"

I told him I could wait. I went over to the door and sat down in a chair to read some magazines.

There were women coming in and out of the shoe store asking for certain sizes, "Do you have this in a five? Do you have this in blue?"

Then I heard another voice.

I heard a voice that said, "Excuse me sir— would you help me please?"

Billy turned around.

I looked up and what did I see? I saw a woman who looked familiar, but I didn't know why.

She turned towards me and that's when I saw it.

I saw a woman with a butterfly tattoo.

Was it her?

I was waiting for Billy to say something to her but he didn't. Billy just walked over to the counter, disappeared behind a curtain, and then re-emerged with a shoe box. He opened them up and showed them to her. He followed her to a seat.

Billy bent down in front of her to put the shoes on her feet. I was waiting for her to say something. Why wasn't she saying anything to him? I was waiting for Rebecca to say something, but she didn't say anything. Why weren't they saying anything?

Was it her?

I didn't even say anything about what happened an hour later when I drove him home.

I asked, "Have you heard anything about what's gonna happen?"

Billy just smiled and said that the lawyer told him it didn't look good. He said they had over half an hour of hidden videos.

Then he chuckled and said, "Yeah, I'm probably going away for awhile."

He was quiet and then he said, "But don't you worry none honey. You'll carry on my memory won't you?"

I didn't answer him.

We didn't say anything else. When we got to his apartment, everything was different than

I imagined. Billy unlocked the door and we went inside.

I thought, "This can't be his apartment?"

There was this wiener dog he had and it had pissed everywhere. It was pissing everywhere now. Everywhere. Billy laughed and didn't even try to stop it. There were pictures of his dead father everywhere. There was a picture of his dead father in the living room. There was a picture of his dead father in the bedroom. There was a picture of his dead father in the bathroom. I looked into the corner and there were piles of clothes everywhere. They were all dirty. There were old dress clothes and suits all dirty and wadded up and wrinkled. Then I saw the desk. It was full of little pieces of paper with phone numbers written on them.

Cynthia 456-8990.

Jenni 456-7850.

Samantha 984-3213.

They were all written in the same hand. They were all written with the same colored ink.

I saw another one that said Rebecca 686-0432.

I told Billy I should be going.

Billy said, "Hey we should go out some-time."

I said, "Yeah let's do that. Give me a call soon."

But I didn't mean it.

And so I left.

Right before I got in my car Billy stuck his head out of the door and he shouted at me, "Hey you know the difference between a dead baby and a rock?"

This time he didn't say the punch line though.

He just looked at me like the punch line was my punch line now, the joke my joke. I heard a conversation from long ago. My friends were... ME.

So even now, years later, I go home now and I hear these jokes. I hear him telling jokes that only I know. I find myself looking into the mirror and I see him. I tighten my tie like Billy tied. I wear dress shirts like Billy used to wear. I look at cash in banks, or cash in offices and dream about stealing it. I look for wallets and

I imagine myself taking them. I see beautiful women and I find myself making up stories about how I fucked them.

I say these stories so many times in my head I wonder, was I there?

Did that happen?

Was it real?

Was she real?

I find myself walking down a hallway and I see Billy. I imagine a whole other life besides my life. People ask me about my life and I lie. I lie because we're all so fucking stupid.

I look into mirrors and I keep saying, "I'm not Billy. I'm Scott. I'm not Billy. I'm Scott. I'm not Scott. I'm Billy. I mean I'm not Billy."

I start telling his jokes in front of people.

I say, "What's the difference between a dead baby and a rock?"

"You can't fuck a rock."

I say, "How do you make a little kid cry twice?"

And then I say the saddest joke of all, the joke we're all afraid to answer.

It's a joke that goes, "Knock knock."

"Who's there?"

"Who?"

"Who Who?"

"Who the fuck knows?"

And you know what?

Nobody laughs.

MARY THE CLEANING LADY

I USED TO STAY with this woman named Mary when I was a little boy. We used to go around Rainelle cleaning houses for people. It was just after my Mom had gone back to work, and she used to carry me into Mary's house before the sun came up. I'd be about half asleep and wrapped in a blanket, and since it was still dark outside she put me on Mary's couch. Then after she left I would watch cartoons on the television and then fall back to sleep dreaming a cartoon dream where I was a cartoon too. And then one morning I woke up and it was time to go cleaning.

Mary said, "Whelp you ready to help me gather up all my cleaning stuff and get going?"

I helped her gather it all up and put it beside the door just like she always did. "And if you're real good today and you don't get afraid then maybe we'll stop by the bus station and get you an ice cream cone."

She smiled and then she said, "I promise it'll go by fast today." Mary was always right. I knew Mary was someone who could control time.

Since she was offering me an ice cream cone to eat, I knew what today was.

It was Wednesday.

Wednesday was the day I dreaded because that's the day we cleaned the monster's house. Now on most days we cleaned nice people's houses—like on Monday we cleaned the house of the little old lady with the shriveled up arm who always tried stuffing my pockets full of whatnots and Hershey Kisses.

On Tuesdays and Fridays we went into Middletown and the welfare apartments and cleaned the house of a woman who had a goiter. I used to dream about popping it with a pin, and wondering if it would deflate like a balloon. The woman with the goiter always smiled at me.

But every other Wednesday we were always cleaning the monster's house, and Mary always bought me ice cream afterwards.

*

Even now I was dreading it, even with the ice cream cone thrown in, even with Mary promising me she would speed up time so it wouldn't take that long. We took off that morning walking through the back alleys of Rainelle, past old shacks built when they were working for Meadow River Lumber company back in the 1930s. And I carried Mary's bucket and mop and held her hand and Mary carried all of her cleaning things with her other hand.

And then she told me about Rainelle.

She told me about how it used to be called Slabtown, and how the new town was built over the old town. She told me if you only dug deep enough there was a whole other town that no one knew about, and was covered up by us all.

She said they even found an old wagon when they built a house 20 years back—houses, streets, covered by these streets, covered by Rainelle.

We walked a bit more.

I imagined this other lumber town covered by Rainelle. I imagined people still living in that town like it was a 100 years earlier and nothing had happened (I imagined even animals walking upright and living like people

live in pants and shirts and walking with walking sticks. It was just like in the cartoons).

Mary said, "Now when we get there you
can just sit on the porch and play with your
cars, but if you get scared and he starts carry-
ing on and trying to fight—you just go outside.
You don't have to stay, all right."

So I shook my head because I knew what kind
of monster it was and I had a whole pocketful
of matchbox cars to keep me busy.

I was just wanting to zip and zap and race
and crash and bash them all together.

I wouldn't even have to think about the monster if I was playing hard enough.

So I held Mary's hand. We turned the corner around the alley and there it was.

It was the monster's house. It was all gray looking and falling down. The paint was chipping
off from where it hadn't been painted in a couple of years. There was an old rusty truck in
the front yard with weeds growing up around
it.

So we clomped up onto the screened in
front porch and Mary knocked.

No one answered.

She put her head inside and knocked again.

No one answered.

She put her head in more and shouted, "I'm here. It's Mary. I'm here to clean for you." She was real careful saying this, even though they took the monster's pistol away a couple of months before.

"I'm here to clean up your toilets and sweep your floor."

And then it was quiet.

And then we heard it.

It was a groan groaning grrrrrrrrrrr-rrrrrrrrrrr like a giant stomach rumbling.

We went inside and I kneeled down on the shut in porch and started playing with my toys.

I imagined the monster's face and the monster's claws. I imagined the monster's smell and the monster's teeth. I imagined the monster eating me, consuming my flesh.

Mary walked into the big room and started talking and getting ready to clean the bathroom with her bucket and her mop.

I sat and took my cars and jumped my cars on the cracked linoleum of the fenced in porch.

I took one of the hot rods and ran it over the crack in the floor.

Then I jumped it—bam.

I took another one and jumped it too. I let them crash into one another, playing death—bam. But after only five minutes of this, I was so bored I couldn't take it anymore. I got up and sat in this old dry rotten chair for awhile and then I got up and walked around the porch.

But then I had an idea.

I wanted to see the monster for myself. I was tired of imagining what he looked like.

After weeks of coming here I'd never seen the monster's face.

So I tiptoed over to where the door was.

And then I looked inside.

I stopped and breathed deep.

Then I looked again.

IT WAS HIM.

But now I could see.

It wasn't a monster.

It was an old man.

He was in a medical bed.

He was all propped up and he had diapers on and a ratty looking t-shirt. He was sitting up. His skull looked like a skeleton skull. He was so skinny he looked like he had a second spine running down the length of his skull. His mouth was open, black and wide and greenish looking and he didn't have any teeth and he was touching his arm and ripping at his chest, whining, "Worms. Worms."

Above him was a clock and it was ticking tick tock, tick tock.

I saw him and he saw me.

I was scared.

So he started shouting dirty words at me like, "Ah shit. You little fucking shit."

Then Mary was back in the room, trying to calm him down. "Now you quit talking filthy like that."

He just kept on. "O god. O god. WORMS. O fucking worms."

So Mary turned towards me and said, "Scott why don't you go ahead and go outside.

We'll be done in a minute."

But I couldn't move.

I was so scared. I stood watching him.

Mary bent over him, whispering, "SHh-hhh."

He moaned, "O god. Fuck. Kill me you bitch."

And then Mary told me to leave again.

I slowly started backing up and listened to the old man moaning, "Fuck."

So Mary looked at me like she meant it this time.

Leave.

So I went outside. I gathered up all of my cars and I went and sat down on the broken concrete steps.

I listened to his moaning and I listened to him groaning, "O god."

And then I heard Mary running the sweeper.

And then the sweeper wasn't sweeping anymore.

And then I heard the whisper again, "O god let me fucking die you bitch."

And then I heard Mary saying, "Now Daddy you quit talking filthy like that. You just quiet down."

And then he was quiet.

I thought to myself, "Daddy?"

What?

Mary cleaned for what would have been about ten or fifteen minutes, but since she told me earlier it would only be a minute, it really only felt like a minute. The minute was up and she came outside. She was smiling. She handed me her bucket and we started walking and holding hands.

She said like nothing had even happened, "Well I guess we need to get this boy an ice cream cone. He did such a good job today. I told you the time would fly by."

And then I grinned and Mary grew quiet.

We walked for a long time in silence.

Mary said, "I'm sorry you had to see that. I'm real sorry."

I said, "Mary is that man really your daddy?"

Mary shook her head "Yes."

I asked, "Well why was he saying all of those bad things?"

We just kept walking and then Mary said, "O he won't be long for this world now. His mind's just eaten up and gone. And the funny thing is he would be so ashamed of himself if he knew he was saying those things. He'd be so ashamed."

So I asked, "Was he a good man Mary?"

Then she chuckled and then she grew quiet again. "Of course he was a good man. He was my daddy."

We walked to the Terminal Drug where the Greyhound bus used to stop in Rainelle. Mary ordered two small vanilla cones for us. We went outside and sat on the sidewalk beneath the old rusty bus sign. Ride Greyhound.

But there wouldn't be any of that today. There would only be the two of us licking our ice cream cones and knowing there were good things in this world too.

It was hard to believe, but there were.

There were good things like ice cream cones, and trying to keep houses clean, towns buried beneath other towns, and your mother bringing you to Mary's house wrapped in a blanket, so you could watch cartoons and dream your cartoon dreams.

And at that moment Mary gave me the ability to control time.

Tick. Tick. Tick.

But sadly, she only taught me how time accelerates, and after all of these years I find I want only the opposite. I only want time to stop. But making it stop is hard and Mary never taught me. Maybe she didn't know herself. But I still must try. So here goes.

Tick Tick Tick.

What's the sound? That's the sound of your heart beating.

Tick Tick Tick.

❋

Close your eyes and please believe me. Close your eyes and and repeat after me.

Time has stopped.

Time has stopped.

TIME HAS STOPPED.

NOW.

A FAREWELL

O but I'm happy to say I'm done with Stories. I learned about life from life itself. Love I learned in a single kiss.

But a few months ago Sarah had a baby—Iris Grace McClanahan.

This is her picture.

There now, even though we are hundreds or thousands of miles apart and have never met you are holding my baby in your hands. Even if this is the future and even if Iris is grown or even gone—she is still here.

You are holding Sarah's baby in your arms.

You are holding the child of Sarah in your hands.

You are holding your own child now.

HAPPY BIRTHDAY!

Scott McClanahan is the author of *Stories* and *Stories II* (published by Six Gallery Press). His other works include *Hill William*, *The Nightmares*, and *Crapalachia* (all forthcoming). He will start writing *The Sarah Book* in 2012. You can watch the films of Holler Presents at: hollerpresents.com.